To: .......................

From: .......................

First published in hardback in Great Britain by HarperCollins Children's Books in 2009
First published in paperback in 2009
This edition published in 2019

1 3 5 7 9 10 8 6 4 2

978-0-00-797699-7

HarperCollins Children's Books is a division of HarperCollins Publishers Ltd.

Text and illustrations copyright © HarperCollins Publishers Ltd 2009

Visit our website at www.harpercollins.co.uk

Printed in China

# If I Were the Easter Bunny

Illustrated by **Louise Gardner**

HarperCollins *Children's Books*

If I were the Easter Bunny,
I'd wake my friends up early.

If I were the Easter Bunny, I'd fill my Easter basket with lots of chocolate eggs...

...and hide them all over the meadow
for everyone to find.

If I were the Easter Bunny,
we'd have a happy hopping competition...

...and an Easter-egg-and-spoon race.
Ready, steady... go!

If I were the Easter Bunny,
we'd make pretty Easter bonnets...

...and I'd lead the way in the **E**aster parade.
Quick, march!

If I were the Easter Bunny,
I'd have a yummy picnic tea...

...and at the end of the day, everyone would go home with a bag of tasty treats.

But, best of all, if I were the Easter Bunny,
I'd save the very last egg, just for…

...ME!
Happy Easter!